Jamakespeare

Brenda Garrick

JACARANDA

This edition first published in Great Britain 2020
Jacaranda Books Art Music Ltd
27 Old Gloucester Street,
London WC1N 3AX
www.jacarandabooksartmusic.co.uk

A CIP catalogue record for this book is available from the British
Library

ISBN: 9781913090166
eISBN: 9781913090364

Cover Design: Rodney Dive
Typeset by: Kamillah Brandes

Printed and bound by CPI Group (UK) Ltd, Croydon, CR0 4YY

For my beautiful Mum and Dad, Eve & Mike

"A formal education will make you a living, self education will make you a fortune."

—Jim Rohn, entrepreneur

Contents

Introduction

When Jacaranda asked me to edit and introduce this ground-breaking collection as part of their Twenty in 2020 series, I was uncertain what I might be able to add. I am conscious that, particularly during this turbulent year that has been 2020 in which we have seen Black and Asian communities disproportionately affected by the Covid-19 pandemic and witnessed sickening examples of the systemic, institutionalised racism that persists, as a white woman my role is to listen to, learn from, and amplify Black voices.

I believe that this collection, full of wit, heart, humour and daring, needs no introduction. The original, amusing, and thought-provoking poetry printed in these pages speaks for itself. Indeed, I would urge the reader to pause reading this introduction now, dive into the poems first and then, if they wish, return to this spot once they have engaged with the texts on their own terms.

Nonetheless, I am grateful and humbled that both Brenda Garrick herself and the team at Jacaranda felt I might be able to offer some thoughts on how this text might be read, particularly among teachers and students of literature. And so it is as a schoolteacher and researcher with an interest in the writing and teaching of multilingual literature that I will endeavour to offer here some musings on the kinds of questions and discussions that might emerge from this collection in the English teacher's classroom.

As any school English teacher knows, the mere mention of Shakespeare will elicit from students a variety of responses, from wide-eyed enthusiasm to breathy trepidation to (dare I admit it?) outright hostility. For many young people, their anxiety or resentment over Shakespeare is expressed in that perennial phrase—*I don't understand.* The language of Shakespeare, unfamiliar and challenging, can too often engender fear and frustration, and yet we still deem the teaching of Shakespeare a core part of English language and literature education. We believe that the struggle to understand pays rewards and, crucially, that learning to grapple with not understanding is a core part of the learning journey.

Still, many young people see Shakespeare as something that isn't for them, belonging to someone else—someone from another time or place or social class. I have always told my students that this is not true: Shakespeare's works belong to anyone who would like to befriend them. However the ways in which Shakespeare is often taught can confirm to many that his works are not accessible, that they are sacrosanct, not to be touched or played with. Valuable projects like the Hip Hop Shakespeare Company, founded by rapper, writer and activist Akala, are sometimes misunderstood as attempts to make Shakespeare 'relevant' to the contemporary young person as if they were a trick, like layering cheese on vegetables to make the salutary palatable. This attitude is rooted in a belief that there are right and wrong (or better and worse) ways to engage with Shakespeare. But Shakespeare does not need to be made relevant. What needs to be made relevant are the ways in which we allow students to respond to and interact with Shakespeare. Art, after all, is there to be reinterpreted and responded to differently as time goes on.

Garrick's collection, *Jamakespeare*, is a powerful example of the joy and creativity to be found in entering into conversation with canonical texts in new ways. With this collection, in which Garrick writes back to Shakespeare's verse in a blend of English and Jamaican Patois, Garrick joins a host of other writers, like John Agard, Valerie Bloom, Linton Kwesi Johnson, Daljit Nagra, and Benjamin Zephaniah, who have written poetry that explores and celebrates the linguistic play that emerges when English blends with 'other' languages,[1] as well as Michael de

---

1 See, for instance, a discussion of Daljit Nagra's poetry in Rachael Gilmour, 'Punning in Punglish, Sounding 'Poreign': Daljit Nagra and the Politics of Lanauage', *Interventions International Journal of*

Souza and Genevieve Webster, the creators of *Rastamouse*, the children's book and television show written in Patois rhyme which was an inspiration for Garrick.

Garrick's poems explore what Mary Louise Pratt first called 'the contact zone', that is, those 'social spaces where cultures meet, clash and grapple with each other, often in contexts of highly asymmetrical relations of power, such as colonialism, slavery, or their aftermaths'.[2] In these pieces Garrick explores the experiences of the Caribbean diaspora in Britain both in the themes and content of the poems but also in the language through which these ideas are conveyed. The reader will encounter a variety of strategies employed to explore what happens in the contact zone between languages, including 'code-switching' (where a speaker moves between one language and another) and orthographic changes (where spellings are amended, especially to capture oral/aural qualities of spoken language).

While the Jamaican Patois might not be familiar to all our students, the questions raised by the language play in *Jamakespeare* will be. There are fruitful and important discussions to be had around the relationship between oral and written language; how the English language has changed (and continues to change) over time, especially as influenced by its contact with the rest of the world's languages; and why so-called 'Standard English' is still disproportionately privileged and valorised, especially in written forms, when most English speakers speak (so-called) 'Non-Standard' forms. For instance, only around 12% of the British population speaks 'Standard English' as their native dialect.[3]

The perpetuation of power structures created by the valorisation of 'Standard English' becomes even clearer when we consider the diverse varieties of English spoken around the

Postcolonial Studies 17 (2014), 686-705.

2 Mary Louise Pratt, 'Arts of the Contact Zone', *Profession* (1991), 33-40 p.34.

3 Peter Trudgill, 'Standard English: what it isn't', in *Standard English: the widening debate*, ed. T. Bex and R. J. Watts (London: Routledge, 1999), 117-128.

world: the English spoken in south London is not the English spoken in Bradford or Glasgow or Lagos or Mumbai or Kingston. Nonetheless our national curriculum for English emphasises the teaching of so-called 'Standard English', defined as 'the variety of English which is used, with only minor variation, as a major world language'.[4] But what kind of English exactly is the 'Standard'? And who gets to determine what language is 'Standard' and what language is Other? It is no surprise that the concept of 'Standard English' aligns itself with centres of power, both within the UK and abroad, in terms of region, nationality, class, wealth, ethnicity and race.

So why perpetuate the idea that one particular version of English is better, more valuable, worthier than others? Not only is this claim that 'Standard English' is the global *lingua franca* a myth—it is also a troubling kind of linguistic imperialism. In recent years, the learning of 'Standard' English has become a dog whistle for right wing, nationalist politics. But the reality is, the United Kingdom is multilingual and increasingly so. Department for Education figures show that one in five state-educated primary-aged children use a language other than English at home and, over time, this figure is increasing.[5] Why, then, are we not making space in our English classrooms to explore what multilingualism means for our young people? Even for children who come from monolingual, Anglophone homes, they are likely engaging in bidialectism, switching between a home dialect and the dialect used at school. The reality, the lived experience of language, is that we are all engaged in heteroglossia, a word translated from the Russian *raznorechie*, coined by the literary theorist Mikhail Bakhtin to capture the concept of 'varied-speechedness' or the linguistic variety that emerges in

4 Department for Education. (2013). 'English programmes of study: key stages 1 and 2 National curriculum in England', September 2013, pp.84-85. Available at: https://assets.publishing.service. gov.uk/government/uploads/system/uploads/attachment_data/file/335186/PRIMARY_ national_curriculum_-_English_220714.pdf

5 Department for Education. (2018). 'Schools, pupils and their characteristics: January 2018', p.10. Available at: https://assets.publishing.service.gov.uk/government/uploads/system/uploads/attach-ment_data/file/719226/Schools_Pupils_and_their_Characteristics_2018_Main_Text.pdf

society.[6] We are all, to at least some extent, heteroglots, varying how we speak depending on our context and interlocutor, whether they be our friend, our teacher, our doctor, our parent, our child. The children we teach will already be skilled in recognising how language changes between the songs they listen to, the discussions they have in the classroom or around the dinner table, and the games they play in the playground.

When heteroglossia is such an important lived reality of language, why then does the national curriculum make so little space for the teaching of multilingual or heteroglossic texts?[7] What is more, there is a strange double standard evident in, on the one hand, celebrating Shakespeare who himself was so playful with language, coining new words and phrases and filling his characters' mouths with puns and malapropisms and, on the other hand, restraining our young people's use of language within the harsh confines of standardised language rules.

Perhaps it is time for a reconceptualisation of language. At present, our education system is founded on a monolingual paradigm, that is, an assumption that we should use *one language at a time*. This paradigm is based on the belief that languages are discrete clearly bounded objects that we can distinguish and name (English vs. French vs. Cantonese vs. Swahili). In fact, we know that languages have blurred edges, blending fluidly into one another. Jamaican Patois is a prime example of this blending, drawing as it does on English and West African languages. Many of us will have experienced the blendedness of languages in our own lives: I, as a Peruvian speaker of Spanish, often find myself able to understand Portuguese, Italian or Chavacano even though, from a monolingual paradigm, I would not be able

6 Mikhail Bakhtin, 'Discourse in the novel' in *The Dialogic Imagination*, ed. Michael Holquist, trans. Caryl Emerson and Michael Holquit (Austin: University of Texas Press, 1981). The translation 'varied-speechdness' is suggested in Martina Björklund, 'Mikhail Bakhtin' in *Philosophical Perspectives for Pragmatics*, ed. Marina Sbisà, Jan-Ola Östman, and Jef Verschueren (Amsterdam: John Benjamins Publishing Company, 2011), 38-52, p.43.

7 A few poems by Nagra, Zephaniah, and Agard feature in some GCSE and A-level anthologies. However, in particular at primary level, the lack of diversity in poetry being studied has been noted by Ofsted—see 'Poetry in schools'. (London: Ofsted, 2007). Available at: https://dera.ioe.ac.uk/7075/8/Poetry_in_schools_(PDF_format)_Redacted.pdf

to claim to speak any of these languages.

The tendency to wish to separate and ring fence named languages descends from the colonial enterprise of approaching the Other with an intention to control. Colonisers approached indigenous peoples, resources, flora, and fauna with the eye of the taxonomist and in separating, describing and classifying they exercised the purported power to name, define and conquer.[8] However there is an alternative way of conceptualising language. Given the complexity of and the blending between languages, it might be more fruitful to think not of *things called languages* but of the *activity of languaging*.[9] Language is not something we *use* but something we *do*, and how we *language* is flexible. Certain kinds of languaging are not, in themselves, more or less valuable than others. Rather, the manner of our languaging gains value from the contexts and purposes in which it is performed and learning to adapt and play with language in these different circumstances is a joyful, wonderful thing.

Jamakespeare is a celebration of heteroglossia and of the playful flexibility of languaging when released from the constraints of standardisation. Spelling is used creatively to capture the way words sound, for instance *duohn* and *rispek*. Early drafts of the poems featured *cos* as a spelling of *because*, but we opted for the less common *kaaz* to capture the elongated vowels of Patois. Astute readers may notice in this collection some variety in the spellings of certain words, like *kyan't* and *carn't* or *tiad* and *taiyad*. These variations are not editorial oversights but rather playful demonstrations of the flexibility of languaging: in the mouths of different speakers, *can't* will be pronounced differently, an aural experience that standardised spellings fail to capture.

The process of editing texts that language beyond the boundaries of 'Standard' language forms is deeply dialogic

8 Johannes Fabian, *Language and Colonial Power: The Appropriation of Swahili in the Former Belgian Congo 19980-1938* (Berkeley: University of California Press, 1986), pp.24-25.

9 Ofelia García, 'Inventing Discourses, Representations and Conceptualizations of Language' in *Disinventing and Reconstituting Languages* ed. Sinfree Makoni and Alastair Pennycook (Clevedon: Multilingual Matters, 2007), xi-xv, p.xi.

and collaborative. This is especially true when the editor is not particularly experienced in the languaging being captured by the texts, as was my case! While Garrick brought to the texts her own personal knowledge of Patois, I was very conscious of my own non-proficiency. In contemplating my editorial suggestions, I found myself regularly reflecting, *Who is the implied reader here? Who are these poems for?* Are these poems written for the fluent speaker of Patois or for a non-Patois speaker? If the former, there is no need in either the writing or the editing to compensate for a potential lack of understanding in the reader. But if the readers are intended to include, for instance, monolingual Anglophones, how much should the texts accommodate these readers' lack of comprehension? Does the writer wish to make understanding harder, emphasising to the monolingual how much they do not know? Or does the writer wish to bridge the gap of understanding between the text and the reader, for instance, with translations, footnotes, glossaries that help the reader access the text? And, in doing so, would the writer find herself merely performing for the Anglophone gaze (or, rather, the Anglophone ear) and perpetuating an Othering of Patois? Even the presence of this introduction, written in academic register and vocabulary, could be seen as a writing to a particular gaze. I hope that this introduction's presence will be interpreted as an act of literary friendliness—an extension of a hand to, especially, those educators who may wish to use these poems with their students but feel they need a little guidance as to the kinds of conversations or lessons that may arise from their use in the classroom.

I sought to edit with a light touch and it was a privilege for me to be able to approach Garrick with questions so that I could better understand her intentions and the languaging being enacted here. I tried to be careful not to rework the language to make it easier to understand for non-Patois speakers, like me, because sometimes the very point of a multilingual, heteroglossic text is to emphasise the gap in understanding between text and reader. In these cases, it is the reader's job to work harder, move in closer. For instance, at times these poems use words that will be strikingly unfamiliar to the non-Patois speaker—words like *nyam*, *duppy* and *pickney* are provided without translation. In providing no footnotes, no glossary, the non-Patois speaker will be faced with her own lack of understanding and will have to make the choice to learn not only what these words mean but also, we hope, their etymologies and histories. In this way, the Anglophone reader experiences a little of the leaning towards that is expected of non-English speakers in nationalistic rhetoric.

Nonetheless there were, during our editorial process, times when we discussed and considered the non-Patois speaker's access to the text, particularly when it came to spellings of words. For instance in 'Names, Nicknames an' Pure Chupidness', we spent a great deal of time puzzling over how to spell *though*. In an early draft, the word was spelled as *dough*, but we mused over whether the denotations of unbaked bread and the associations with the slang term for 'money' might clutter the line with unwanted imagery and connotations. Alternative spellings created similar problems: *doe* (a female deer) and *doh* (too reminiscent of Homer Simpson) offered little assistance. In 'If Summer be Di Season', we also pondered over *bun* (as in *burnt*). I was concerned that *bun food* would be read, by the monolingual Anglophone, as meaning bread buns, particularly given that the poem is set at a barbecue. But when I understood that there was no other spelling that could capture the phonetics of the sound of the adjective *burnt* in Patois, we concluded that perhaps these instances of meanings becoming lost in translation were part of the point of these poems. When we engage in languaging across contact zones and linguistic boundaries, there may be times of miscommunication or comprehension gaps, but these do not need to be a source of strife.

Readers may also note that apostrophes to denote contractions, omitted or added letters are not applied strictly consistently across the collection. Again, this is an intentional rejection of standardisation of rules even across the collection itself, let alone across a whole dialect or language. There were instances where we considered the apostrophe helpful to the reader to distinguish a word from potential homonyms—*h'eight* (eight) vs. *height* or *h'eat* (eat) vs. *heat*. There were other instances where altering how an end consonant was used or dropped varied because of the desired sound of a line: in 'Turn Down di TV', the first *what* is a *wha'* while the second is a *what*, the final 't' retained for its plosive effect at the end of the sentence. Of course, oftentimes, these apostrophes become irrelevant when the poem is performed orally, and to Garrick, an actor herself, the oral performance of these poems is of crucial importance. As Garrick often commented to me, Shakespeare's plays were written to be spoken and to be heard. The same is true of the verses in this collection.

As central as the oral/aural is to this collection, to Shakespeare's works, and to poetry in general, there is something important about printing multilingual, bidialectical and 'non-Standard' works on the page. Printing, publishing, disseminating, and teaching these texts is a demonstration that we value them and that we deem their languaging valid and beautiful. I hope that this collection will help highlight the need for further published works celebrating the diversity of languaging that takes place in Britain. There is space in our classrooms, in our bookstores, and in our public spaces for a plurality of voices. And if you, when this diversity of voices is amplified, find yourself a little bewildered, not understanding the languaging you are hearing, know that part of the education of that experience is to learn to sit with not understanding—to listen, to acknowledge your own fear or frustration if they arise, but to continue to listen anyway. And, through listening, you may come to find that you understand more than you thought you would.

Karina Lickorish Quinn

A Note from the Author

My first foray into the world of William Shakespeare was, as Karina Lickorish Quinn states in her introduction, 'outright hostility.' That may be a strong statement, but I wasn't keen. I struggled with the language, prose and poetry, and thought, if you want to communicate just talk plainly. I couldn't visualise people conversing in long monologues! However, Shakespeare sprung into life when I saw my first play, *Macbeth*, set in contemporary England where the witches were drug-induced psychics. I was hooked—Shakespeare can be relevant and is universal.

I wrote these poems, which I view as monologues/soliloquies, to be performed as an homage to the oral tradition of the Caribbean and Africa. I relish the rhythms, sounds and playfulness of Patois from Grenada and Jamaica: take, for instance, the Patois word 'facety' for the English 'facetious'. I had a light bulb moment when I discovered at university that Patois is recognised as an official language. I found this empowering and want to pass the mantle onto anyone who reads this collection to write poems in their vernacular that relates to their heritage and upbringing.

Brenda Garrick

Is dis a Pattie?

Is dis a pattie which mi see before mi?
Come, let mi nyam thee,
di answer to mi belly.
Come 'ere nah man!
Mi 'ave de not, yet mi crave de still.
Why unnu like fi torment mi so?
Yu treating mi bad man,
mi belly gripe mi for true.
Is yu a figment of I n I imagination?
But wait! Wha' yu ah say?
Mi still see yu—
A yu dat drag me 'ere y'know!
Mi lef' mi rice n peas... chicken... dumplin'... plantain...
Chah nah man, mi gone!

To Swim or not to Swim

now dat is de problem!
Wedder 'tis nobler to wash miself before or afta—
before duohn mek sense!
To drown, perchance to float,
now dat is I n I vexation;
is it becos I n I is Black?
Mi heritage, mi ball an' chain
dat me carn't tread 'pon de water?
But wha gwaan?
De water is nah mi friend, mi bredrin.
Mi hair ah shrink up,
mi skin ah quail up,
yu know wha sah man.
Swimming is for de birds!
Pass mi di cocoa butter, yu hear?
I goin' for a sea-bart!

Di'airdresser

If we 'airdressers 'ave offended,
tink but dis an' all is mended
dat unnu did sojourn 'ere…

Di 'airdressee

sojourned! Yuh call dat sojourned?
Yuh mean tell mi dat being 'ere h'eight long, dry 'ours
to do one likkle ting,
to di caca coco 'pon me 'ead should take dat long?
Unno playing di arse!
It quicker to fly foreign an' see me sistren inna New York
dan do me 'air,
but me ah held captive under di dryer
wid no nourishment, no refreshments,
nah even wahn bed to lie 'pon.
It come like being a guest at 'er Majesty's
mi gwan shave mi 'air all off, Yul Bryner stylee
so mi can just, wake up an' mi gone!

Di 'airdresser
So wha' yuh 'ave plan fi di rest ah di day?

Di 'airdressee
Mi go ah tell 'er one bad word yuh see!

But Stop!

But stop! Who wastin' mi 'lectric?
Oho it di lovebirds-dem.
Switch it off! Yu pay di bills?
What mi waahn know is
what wrong wid di sun?
Or di moon for dat matter?
It plenty bright.
Why unnu lovers like fi woo
one anudder in di dark anyhow?
Yu nyam carrot or what?
An' why shi upstairs?
An' him down di road?
Dem kyan talk to one anudder?
Dem kyan hug an' kiss-up?
Anyhow, mi know de yut' dem love fi text—
Now what chupidness is dat!
I need nuttin' to talk, yu know.
I is a master communicator, sah,
Me! I talkin' an' makin' noise 'til the day I drop.
Bwouy, yut' wasted on di pickney-dem.

Turn Down di TV

Turn down, turn down di TV man
an' 'top yer noise!
Wha' yu a frighten mi for?
Yu wan' bus' mi eardrums?
Why is it that when cricket or boxing is on, yu turn too good
for nuttin'?
Days yu spend in front of di TV
cocking up yur foot,
wid yur rum or Special Brew
like yu is som king
an' it not jus' yu!
Unnu good for nuttin' frien' jus' come an' plant demselves in
front of di TV,
nyamin' food an' drink like it gone outta fashion.
Well it nah go so!
Don't hush mi! Yu waahn mi fi cuss some bad words?
It mus' be a man who invented di Ashes.
Four weeks ah pure man chupidness…
But, but, but di idea, a bomb hit mi kitchen?
Lord God, mi heart carn't tek dis,
Mi sick an' taiyad…
Mi do what? Mi look like slave to unnu?
Jus' move yuh backside in 'ere right now!

Smart Phones

To have no screen…
Smart Phone, what!?
Dey can work fi demselves?
Dey still need some dumb unnu to work dem
Check dis—smart phones ah make unnu chupid
How yu mean yu h'allow ah piece a sup'm to take hova unnu
life?
When to get up, when to sleep, when to go fi ah run, wha'
unnu Fido now?
Smart phone ah tell unnu wha' di wedder gwan do?
Di Hinglish wedder h'is one 'ell of ah ting to predict.
Why unnu nah look outta yuh window or jus' look h'up!
Unnu mus' swipe lef', swipe right, 'ell no, unnu mus' LOOK
right, LOOK lef' or wahn piece ah cyar go lik unnu duohn!
Di Almighty nah put mi 'pon dis 'ere h'eart' fi look duohn 'pon
di screen 24/7, mi 'ave a life!!!
Wha' ihm say? Internet?
Internah mi sah.

Outta Mi Window

But wait! Yu gat someone fi tell unnu
fi look out unnu window?
Wha' di hell ah gwan in dis 'ere Hingland!
Mi look chupid to yu?
Mi know wha' di window is far, too rhaatid!
Wha' mi see…
Foxes done take hover mi backyard—dem pay rent?
'Nough time me does chase dem dutty h'animal outta mi
garden.
Dem 'ave no rispek, just come shit-up in mi vegetables h'and
flowers-bed.
Dem lucky mi nah 'ave no gun fi blast dem inna dem backside!
Or a cutlass fi chop dem 'ead off!
And why Hingland like fi paint up dem road, sah?
White line 'ere, yellow line dere an' red!
Wha' dis is, rainbow city?
Now mi vex long time cos dem put white line outside mi
yard—
Dey wan' mi pay fi park h'outside mi front door?
Wha' craziness is dis?
I giving dem one cuff inna dem 'ead!
Mi nah shack-up inna cyar park!
Back 'ome mi nah need no window, mi 'ave a verandah:
mi see di coconut trees, palm trees while mi drink some
fire-water,
steelpan ah playin' sweet tunes inna de distance—
But wait! Who let de Trini's in?
Done mess-up mi dream!

Traffic Wardens

What godforsaken planet dese people drop from?
Dey on di road 24/7, mi nah see dem sleep, mi nah see dem
h'eat, nah h'even go fi a comfort break?!
Mi nah even see dem before dem ah strike, dem like di silent
ninja stalker!
Swif' an' deadly!
Dem 'ave no 'eart, no mercy,
jus' slap a ticket 'pon me car.
Yu kyan't say 'boo', 'ooo', 'mi sorry'—nuttin'!
Jus' wan second! Wan second, mi late!
An' dem stand dere wid a face favour Smiley Culture
(more like face favour Satan!)
enjoying di misery dem inflict 'pon mi
wid wahn piece a paper,
wahn piece a paper dat will cost me h'over £100!
Dat seem fair to unnu?
Dem kyan't ketch terrorists but dey kyan ketch h'innocent ol' mi
wid a parking ticket!
Mi look like wahn criminal to unnu?
Hm. Traffic wardens,
spiteful dem spiteful yu see!

Names, Nicknames, an' Pure Chupidness!

Beg pardon?
Wha' yu ah say yu name is?
Di question mi 'ave to ask all di while,
where di 'ell dey get dese names from?
Di parents smoke ganja or get one lash inna
dem 'ead dat it turn dem fool-fool?
Now I is a travelling man, but mi never meet an Apple.
Is dat a name—an' fi a gal?
But wha' di backside!
Eh, mi lookin' for 'er brudda, Pineapple…
Yu see 'im dere?
Now mi 'ave a bredrin call Stretcho, an' one name Cockeye,
an' mi bes' pardner Sodium but it nah appear on dem
birt' certificate!
Dey call me Kiddyman, cos mi likes a joke;
Mi 'ave a good, strong Jamaican name, Cedric—
Mi great, great, Granfarder name.
Look 'ere now mi always dream mi 'ave
a flash kyaar. But mi brokes!
So mi tell di wife, she 'ave fi drop anudder pickney.
It 'ave to be a girl doah,
An' when me frien' dem arsk "wha' she ah call?"
Mi can say dat: "Me 'ave a Mercedes!"

If February be di Month ah Love

If February be di month ah love,
mi know! Mi look chupid to yu?
Dey does ram it down mi troat all di while!
It all h'over di damn place.
It come di same time h'every year, di same ole ting an' ting,
di same ole story.
Red rose-dem appear in di middle ah winter,
where dey come from?
Perfume done stuff up mi nosehole.
Choke dem ah try an' choke mi!
An' de amount ah chocolate I does see in di shop-dem,
entice dey waahn to entice me.
I jus' spend di last six weeks after Christmas try
to lose mi love 'andles-dem!
In my day, Valentines was 'bout sending a card to a gal
(tuu if yu greedy).
Now unnu 'ave fi wine an' dine 'er, buy card, chocolate,
perfume
an' wait fi it… a teddy bear,
an' it mus' be pink to rhatid!
Mi look like millionaire to unnu?
Anyhow, mi wifey does say Valentines
should be ah heveryday kinda bizniz.
Me kyan 'andle dat…
(long as it take place inner di bedroom,
yu get me!)

Passion

Passion, what is passion?
No budder h'ask mi!
I is a champion lover—
dey does call me Sagger Bwoy.
Mi 'ad passion before I could walk,
before I could talk—
Di girls, dem love me to rhaatid.
Yu know say whey Grace Jones dedicate a tune fi me?
My Jamaican Guy
It's mi she ah sing about!
Yu know sometin'?
I n I was born ready;
I could sweet talk dem girl-dem
from di time I inna mi nappy, no wait, inna di womb!
James Brown no know what 'im talk 'bout:
Sex Machine, mi, I n I h'is a sex h'industry!
Mi soon go global an' trade 'pon di Stock Market.
Den h'everibadi can 'ave a piece ah mi,
Seen!

Mi Lef' No Ring

Mi lef' no ring wid her
Wha shi ah talk about?
Mi know mi good lookin!
A feast for unnu eyes,
but mi lady ah talk nonsense.
She luv me fi true, she carn't help it,
mi know I n I is di man
but me feel sorry fi her
kaaz she better off if I wahn figment of 'er imagination—
a duppy no less.
What ah gwaan in di ladies' heart-dem?
Lord ah mercy, dem too fool-fool yu see.
Me get married & tie de knot? Yu mus be mad!
Yu wan mi fi dead!

Mi Lef' No Ring (Part 2)

Mi lef' no ring wid her,
wha' ihn ah talk 'bout?
Is it mi Brocade
dat sweet her so?
Or mi funky dread-dem
that seduce her?
Mi know mi look good as a man
but mi lady ah talk nonsense!
Mi Master sent her no ring
I n I is de man!
It's mi Master she waahn, not mi.
Mi feel sorry fi her
bekaaz shi better off if I is a mirage.
What ah go on in de lady 'eart-dem?
Lord ah mercy, dem too fool-fool yu see!
What a ting!
Mi Master love her, I love 'im
an' shi love mi—mess commess!
Mi carn't fix this;
Only time will tell if mi plan a backfire.

50 Shades ah Nastiness

Knowing 'ow mi love mi books,
mi 'usband buy mi one 'bout
artists, ah so mi taught.
Now mi know nuttin' 'bout art, but mi loves to read.
Well, lawdamercy! Mi eyes dem ah pop outta mi 'ead.
Mi lost fi words h'and mi get so hot, mi 'ave fi take cold
showers!
H'every page mi ah turn is full ah nastiness.
H'every word mi ah read is full ah duttiness.
But yu know something—
Mi kyan't put di damn book down!
H'every minute ah h'everyday, I readin':
in di bedroom, in di toilet, on di train,
mi no care who see mi—mi loves it!
Mi never feel so alive, so sexy!
Mi learn some new moves to try wid mi 'usband
but 'im kyan't keep up, so mi lef 'im!
Mi now 'ave mi own fifti shades ah sexiness,
mi own fifti shades ah grey.
I mus' tank de autor, she change mi life,
an' I taught toys were honly fi di pickney-dem.
Mmmmm, life—it sweet.

If Summer be di Season ah Carnival

If summer be di season ah Carnival… Play Mas!
I done ready to whine up mi waist behind some
pretty gal inner 'er bikini. Mi no fussy.
Mi nah know how dem gal-dem does get away wid
dancing 'alf naked.
But mi no care, Christmas come h'early!
Sometimes mi does get carry away, jumpin'
up and whinin',
an' somebaddy mash me foot
an' mi 'ave fi say sorry!
What kinda liberation is dat? It fair, hm!
Yu tink if mi wear white or red shoes, dey'll see me
toes dem, nah mi neider!
Yu know di best ting 'bout Carnival, it not di
calypso music, nor di sweet smelling food…
it di after-party! Mi jus ah love freeness.
An' when mi get in dere an' mi start fi sweat—
It hot, hot, hot fi true!

One More Chune!

Wan more chune, DJ Selector, wan more.
Dem reggae chune dey play dere, nice yu see.
Mi like fi fling foot 'pon di dancefloor:
I n I is a tiger, yu know.
Don't give me no calypso or soca doah,
mi whinin' days is h'over.
It done mash-up mi waist,
an' mi love fi see di ladies-dem.
Dey like fi daizzle-up demselves:
hours dem spend putting on dem make-up—an' for what?
Only to see the sweat jus' take it off, one time hey, hey.
One dance wid me an' dem clothes jus' fly off, two time.
Yu see me, I press dem 'pon de wall jus' so an'... anyhow
Eh! But wait yu nah hear me, Mr DJ?
Me nah talk to miself yu know,
mi say, REWIND!

If Summer Be Di Season

If Summer be di season ah barbecue,
bring it on! I 'ungry!
Gimme meat, meat, meat all di time.
Me carn't eat food widout meat:
unnu wan' kill me!
Man, mi love fi see di chicken, ribs, an' beef
jus' sizzle 'pon di fire;
di smell does sweet mi mout' yu see.
But make sure yu get dere before Usain Bolt Mary:
she fat like dumplin' but 'er titty-dem flat like pancake!
(A joke me ah joke!)
Anyhow, she nyam food like it ah go outta fashion.
Shi eye bigger dan shi belly.
Velma say she eatin' fi de five-touzand, an' mi can well see dat!
And who invite 'enry?
'enry nah eat no meat!
Give 'im a plate ah roast corn an' 'im belly full.
But 'im margar, yu see—sneeze an' 'im fall h'over!
No worry, mi still loves 'im like cooked food.
Talkin' ah food, me check yu later;
mi dead fi 'ungry an' mi nah like bun food!

Tofu or not Tofu

Dat is not a question,
in dis or h'any udder lifetime!
Yu wan' me fi choose
between wahn juicy piece ah chicken breast
or wahn anaemic piece ah cardboard?
No contes'!
Tofu 'ave no salt, no taste, no texture,
it nah meat, it nah vegetable,
yu can season it 'til kingdom come
an' it still 'ave no flavour.
It come like castor oil for di veggie people-dem
kaaz yu mus' 'ave fi 'old unnu nose to swallow it!
Tofu? Toe who?

Now it October an' it Black History Month

Now it October an' it 'Black History Month'
an' I vex, vex, vex!
How kyan yu squeeze a whole heap ah Black History
into one month is beyond a joke!
Dem facety 'ee!
Mi 'ave fi go 'ere, dere an' h'everywhere.
What, yu tink me is, butter dat I can spread miself over
de whole ah London?
Mi 'ead ah 'urt me, jus' tinking 'bout it!
Mi 'ead ah spin wid all de tings dat ah gwaan.
Black History should be an h'everyday kinda business, sah!
If somebaddy say to unno dat dey nah 'ave no
White History month, so why dem 'ave Black History month
tell dem dey do—
it call 'History'. FULL STOP!

All Hallow's Eve

Nack! Nack! Nack!
Who di hell wanna lik dung mi door at dis h'unearthly 'our?
Do dem see wahn light in yonder window break?
NO!
Mi make sure mi turn off all di lights an' di TV inna mi yard
an' yet mi still hear di gate jus' swing h'open, di footstep-dem
come up mi stairs and di rhaatid doorbell ah ring!
Who dem tink mi is—Dracula?

Nack! Nack! Nack!
Who di 'ell wahn bata dung mi door?
All yu parents wicked 'ee!
Di pickney should be in dere bed, snuggled up wid teddy,
not nacking 'pon mi door,
walking di streets begging fi sweets.
Unnu nah 'ear, sweet-dem bad fi unnu teet!
Gwaan, di dentist 'ave all 'im sharp tools waiting fi unnu—
jus' 'ave unnu bank kyaad ready!

Now is di Winter

Now is di Winter of wi discontent?
It nah mine, mi nah ask for it!
Who in dem right mind would ask fi snow?
Soft and fluffy, no sah man—
it cole like hell!
Mi nose a run, mi feet come like popsicles,
mi kyan't feel dem.
Mi ah ketch a fall all di time.
Me nah fair better in di English Summer;
how di sun kyan shine but it nah warm unnu?
It a joke—four season-dem in wan day!
Mudda Nature, yu can keep yu English wedder;
mi never leave mi hot country to come live in wahn ice-box!
Mi ah go home, back-ah-yard!

Look 'pon di Queen

It look ah bit shady...
Murray ah win Wimbledon h'after sevnti-sevn years.
Mi did watch di match
wid mi own h'eyes,
but mi ah go eye doctor tomorrow fi real!
Mi kyan't believe it!
Yu waahn know what I tink?
Yu waahn know what I feel?
Obea! Obea!
Now mi don't believe in such tings,
'ow wan person can do voodoo an' change 'istory,
change unnu's destiny...
uh uh, no wan person kyan 'ave such power.
But mi ah say to unnu, look 'pon di Queen!
Check dis out, when Virginia Wade win ah Wimbledon in
nainteen sevnti-sevn,
h'it was di Queen's Silver Jubilee.
When Murray did win, h'it shi sixti year Coronation...
Sevnti-sevn year since Perry win, dere's dat number again
Obea! Obea!
Look 'pon di Queen,
wan dangerous lady, trus' me!

Windrush

London is di place for me,
dum, du-u-um, dum, di dum, di dum;
London, dis lovely city
dum, du-u-um, dum, di dum, di dum.
Wha' lovely 'bout it?
When mi come to Hingland
it cole to rhaatid!
An' di people-dem cole like di wedder!
But wait, is dem not h'invite unnu
dem seh, 'di Mudder country needs yu?'
Is dat di way to treat unnu guests?
No dogs! No Irish! No Blacks!
Facety dem facety.
Mi? Mi come fi make mi fortune in faiv short years,
an' go back in mi yard.
Huh, faati-tuu long, hard years later mi still 'ere.
Where di 'ell di time go, eh?
An' yu know sup'm, mi still ah go seek mi fortune!
Life inna Hingland nah h'easy, believe!
Mi 'ave Teddy Boys waahn beat mi h'every night an' day,
mi 'ad wahn woman throw water 'pon mi cos mi 'ad de auda-
ciousness to shelter from di rain inna shi porch,
but wi do dis back home, no problem.
Wi should get wahn medal for di liberties di h'Inglish take 'pon
wi Black people.
Yu tink I fair better back 'ome?
I seen as wahn foreigner in Hingland,
back 'ome dey treat mi like wahn tourist!
Mi go buck-up inna di sea,
create mi h'own h'island,
mi h'own likkle paradise!
Di worse dat can 'appen is mi drown or
wahn shark nyam up mi backside!

43

Di Windrush Scandal ('Ostile Enivronment)

To live in London yu are really comfortable
dum di dum di dum di dum
because di Hinglish people are very sociable.
Dey take yu 'ere h'and dey take yu dere
and make yu feel like a millionaire…
Well, well, well…
Hingland in di '40s was wahn hostile place,
sevnti years later, nuttin ah change—it still 'ostile!
How kyan di British Gouvament,
di *civilised* British Gouvament
turn roun' an' say we kyan't stay 'ere?
Dey lose mi papers, I lose mi job.
Mi British passport nah wort de paper it printed 'pon,
Mi lose di house mi get from mi Pardner.
It no matter dat mi work 'ere fi h'over faati years,
mi family born 'ere, school 'ere,
dey marry 'ere an' 'ave dem own pickney,
an' yet still dem say, I is an *h'illegal h'immigrant*!
So mi life is jus' wahn illusion to dem?
Di Gouvament waahn h'offer £50K for di stress dem cause?
It should be £150K!
How can dey compensate for di trauma ah going in an' out an'
out an' in ah di detention centre?
Treated like ah criminal,
no better dan a dawg…

Brexit

Once more unto di voting boot' mi bredrin, once more.
Yu nah tiad?
Wha' ah gwaan inna di British people head-dem?
H'everybady jump 'pon di crazy train—
"Let's get our country back!"
Whom Hingland belong to anyhow? Nah wi, nah dem.
Dis country been invaded since di dawn ah time!
Di country don't belong to h'enibadi!
H'evribadi is an h'immigrant 'ere.
£350M to de NHS—ha!
Bo Jo turn yu all fool-fool!
All foreigners 'ave fi go home—which 'ome?
Dis is me 'ome: I born 'ere.
So yuh nah get rid ah me dat easy.

Is dis a virus?

'Ello, wha' fresh 'ell is dis?
Is dis a virus which mi ah see before mi?
Come, let me flee de, mi 'ave di not—GOOD!
Mi nah wahn fi dead yet!
Who or what ah try h'an murder mi?
It start 'ow many miles from mi yard?
An' h'overnight h'it h'end up right under mi nose-hole.
Wha' ah gwan wid Mudder H'eart'? Pandemonium!
Mi did know dis virus nah ramp
when Maccy D's hand Primani ah shutdown.
Lawdamercy, tings-dem ah start fi vanish—
hand-gel, wha' wrong wid soap n water?
Toilet roll, 'ow big is unnu battam?
Den flour, h'eggs an' sugar—hmmm!
H'all mi ah say is look 'pon unnu waistline…
Mi! Mi kyan't take dis social distance.
Mi ah use a tape measure inna di bedroom
h'and mi ah fall off di bed.
H'it nah go work!

Mr Lightning Bolt

Lawd Gad, mi sad yu see.
Bolt ah retire—at thirti!
Mi go miss 'im,
'ow dat man bring sunshine inna mi life,
joy inna mi soul—
'hw 'im do dat?
'Im funny, 'im talented an' 'im fast,
blink an' 'im gone, in 9.58 seconds!
World class!
Mi barely knows 'im but mi loves 'im.
Mi could watch 'im fi 'ours
like wahn gazelle inna di savannah,
a country mile ahead ah di competition,
wahn icon an' enigma, wahn true legend!
Di h'end of an era.
Di h'end of mi long distance love affair…

Mr Bolt Lightning

Bolt! But wha' di...?
Caca Faat!
Mi did know someting was wrong wid yu!
Yu come to di championships looking rough,
didn' yu resign las' year?
Yuh hair nah cut,
yuh beard nah shave,
yu look heavy, nah swif' like an arrow—
more heavy like dumpling!
Mi nerves kyan't take dis!
Mi done wid love,
di affair is h'over!
Why yu nah listen an' stop after Rio?
Yuh head too hard!!!

Guess What Mi Is?

If reincarnation heggist,
mi know what mi wanna be next time roun'—
di ultimate stalker
dat hattack from di back,
mi follow unnu to di h'ends ah de h'eart'—
mi loyal dat way,
like a silent ninja.
I'll stan' guard roun' yu bed,
mi nah go nowhere.
Mi stick to unnu like superglue.
Mi ah serenade unnu while unnu sleep.
Wan ting, jus' wan ting me waahn…
unnu sweet Hinglish blood!

If We Rastas Have Offended

If we Rastas have offended,
good! What yu ah look 'pon mi for?
Yu too dyamn fas'—
mi look like h'entertainer to yu?
Yu have fi 'fraid Babylon, nah mi.
I n I locks might favour lion
but it nah bite yu, ah so mi ah stay.
Is lie mi ah lie? No sah man,
it di trut' mi ah talk.
I n I is jus' a natural man, yu know,
livin' off de land, h'eating ital food,
smokin', di 'oly 'erb, dreamin' of di 'omeland.
Ever fait'ful, ever trut'ful
A Rastaman never dies
Rastafari vibrations,
feelin' irie! Feelin' high!
I Selassie I! Jah Rastafari!

Shakespearean References

Poems are listed in alphabetical order by their title.

50 Shades ah Nastiness

The Tempest
I:ii 'Knowing I love my books'

All Hallow's Eve:

Macbeth
II:iii 'Knock knock knock'

Brexit
One More Chune!

Henry V
III:i 'Once more unto the breach'

But Stop!

Romeo and Juliet
II:ii 'But soft! What light…'

Di 'airdresser

A Midsummer Night's Dream
V:i 'If we shadows…'

If February be di Month
ah Love
If Summer be di Season…

Twelfth Night
I:i 'If music be the food of love'

If We Rastas Have Offended

A Midsummer Night's Dream
V:i 'If we shadows…'

Is dis a Pattie?
Is dis a Virus?

Macbeth
II:i 'Is this a dagger'

Look 'pon di Queen:

Hamlet
V:ii 'Look to the Queen'

Mi Lef' No Ring (I & II)	*Twelfth Night* II:ii 'I left no ring with her'
Names, Nicknames…	*Romeo and Juliet* II:ii 'Tis but thy name…'
Now is di Winter Now it October…	*Richard III* I:i 'Now is the Winter of our Discontent'
Smart Phones	*The Tempest* I:ii 'To have no screen'
Tofu or not Tofu To Swim or not to Swim	*Hamlet* III:i 'To be or not to be'
Turn Down di TV	*Richard III* I:ii 'Set down, set down…'

Bibliography

Bennett, Louise, (1993) *Aunty Roachy Seh*, Sangster's Book Stores Ltd

The Cambridge Text, *The Complete Works of William Shakespeare*, The Octopus Group Ltd

Zahl, Peter-Paul, (2003) *Anancy Mek It*, LMH Publishing Ltd, Jamaica

Acknowledgements

Much love and appreciation to:

The Posse* for being the initial inspiration as to why I wrote the first poem; I was writing this material for them to perform. Sadly The Posse is no more, but I enjoyed many a performance in the 1990s; I laughed 'til mi belly bus!'

Louise Bennett whose writings put Jamaican Patois (Patwah) on the map and may have been influential in this language being officially recognised.

Bob Marley for his inspirational music and lyrics.

The Lewisham Library Writers' Group and Verna Wilkins (for setting up this group). This group was and still is a great support, encouraged me to write more poems and inspired some of the subjects. The first poem had been languishing in the bottom of my drawer for over ten years!

My friends, family and hairdresser for listening to my poems and their welcome feedback, both negative and positive. To Gary Gillet in Maui for the title and for making me LOL when he did a Jamaican accent. Americans aren't known for their accents—*Cool Runnings*, *Oceans 11* and *Mary Poppins* come to mind (I won't name the guilty culprits) but there are a few exceptions (Gwyneth Paltrow, Renée Zellweger).

Vivienne Rochester for staging some of my poems at the City Literary Institute.

My Mum and Dad for putting up with me, my dreams and

not having a proper job. On their first exposure to my writing, both parents were complimentary, saying that I could make some money from my work. On the second hearing, my Mum said,"Gyal, what stupidness yu write dere!"

My guardian angel, Frank, Archangels Michael (for courage) and Gabriel (for my creativity) for being with me every step of the way.

David Garrick (an 18th century actor) who put Shakespeare's hometown on the map with a three-day festival and popularised the Bard once more.

I'd like to thank the Don that is William Shakespeare—what more can I say, for without him this body of work wouldn't exist!

Muchas Gracias Karina, mi hermosa amiga for doing such a stellar job in editing Jamakespeare! Thanks for agonising, deliberating over this book with your delicate touch; I now appreciate how editing is a labour of love and I felt yours in abundance. I wasn't expecting such a well thought out, academic and in-depth introduction. Thank you for accepting this challenge—Estaré para siempre en tu deuda!

Last but not least, I will be forever indebted to Jacaranda Books for choosing to publish my poems by being part of the cohort that is Twenty in 2020. Thank you Valerie, Jazzmine, Mags, Cherise and all the staff at Jacaranda who are responsible for validating my dream of being an author—I have arrived!'

*aka Brian Bovell, Michael Buffong, Victor Romero Evans, Robbie Gee, Roger Griffiths, Gary McDonald, Eddie Nestor, Sylvester Williams

About the Author

Brenda Garrick was born of Grenadian parents, not Jamaican as you might suspect. She was born, bred and is living in London, UK.

Since Brenda was a child, she has always written; as a consequence, she relished the English side of her BA at the University of Roehampton more than the Drama module!

She discovered whilst writing these poems her alto-ego is a grumpy, old Jamaican man.

Brenda is currently rewriting a Shakespearean play into Jamaican patois, a historical play about a female hero and writing stories for children.